# One Good Deed

This
**PJ BOOK**
belongs to

_____

_____

JEWISH BEDTIME STORIES and SONGS

To Ashley and Tyler Malkin and Skyler Fields
and to their mommies and daddies who are
helping them become such amazing people.
And to Barbara Bernstein who embodies
kindness in the world.—T.F.

Text copyright © 2015 by Terri Fields
Illustrations copyright © 2015 by Deborah Melmon

KAR-BEN PUBLISHING
A division of Lerner Publishing Group, Inc.
241 First Avenue North
Minneapolis, MN 55401 USA
1-800-4-KARBEN

Website address: www.karben.com

Main body text set in Handy Sans. 18/22.
Typeface provided by MADType.

Library of Congress Cataloging-in-Publication Data

Fields, Terri, 1948-
    One good deed / by Terri Fields ; illustrated by Deborah Melmon.
        pages    cm
    Summary: A young boy transforms his neighborhood by performing one good deed for his
neighbor, which leads to a chain of kind and helpful actions.
    ISBN: 978-1-4677-3478-3 (lib. bdg. : alk. paper)
    [1. Conduct of life—Fiction.  2. Kindness—Fiction.  3. Helpfulness—Fiction.  4. Neighbors—
Fiction.]  I. Melmon, Deborah, illustrator.  II. Title.
PZ7.F479180n 2015
[E]—dc23                                                    2014028814

Manufactured in Hong Kong
1 - PN - 9/1/15

011613.2K1/B0756/A5

# One Good Deed

Terri Fields

Illustrated by
Deborah
Melmon

KAR-BEN
PUBLISHING

Even on sunny days, Lancaster Street seemed dark and gloomy. Neighbors did not smile at each other...or talk to each other...or help each other.

But one day, as Jake climbed his mulberry tree to pick its ripe fruit, he saw old Mrs. Thompson outside her house next door.

Suddenly he had a thought he'd never thought before.
I bet she's sad she can't climb trees. I could take her
some of these delicious mulberries.

When Jake arrived, Mrs. Thompson was surprised. She was delighted. She had enough fruit to make two mulberry pies.

Then she had a thought she'd never thought before. *I loved getting these mulberries. I bet Mr. Riley next door would like one of my pies.*

When Mrs. Thompson arrived, Mr. Riley was surprised. Mr. Riley was delighted. As he ate the delicious pie, he looked out the window and watched the kids next door playing ball. Suddenly he saw the ball land on the roof of his garage.

Then he had a thought he'd never thought before. *I bet I could help them. I could take* my *ladder and get their ball.*

When Mr. Riley handed them back their ball, Jeffrey and Joshua were surprised. They were delighted. As they tossed it back and forth, they saw Mr. Lee hobbling on crutches to his front door.

Then they had a thought they'd never thought before. *Mr. Lee can't rake the leaves in his yard. But we could!*

When the boys arrived with their rakes, Mr. Lee was surprised. Mr. Lee was delighted. Soon they were joined by Sammy Cohen from next door carrying a rake. "My computer is broken, so I can't finish my homework. I'll help you rake."

Then Mr. Lee had a thought he'd never thought before.
*I'm good at computers. Maybe I could fix Sammy's computer.*

When Mr. Lee arrived, the Cohens were surprised. The Cohens were delighted and before you knew it, the computer was up and running again.

When Mrs. Cohen sat down to check her
e-mail, she looked out her window and saw
Ashley from next door, riding a rusty old bike.

Then she had a thought she'd never thought before. We have a practically new bike that **Sammy** has outgrown. It would be perfect for **Ashley**.

When Mrs. Cohen arrived with the new bike, Ashley was surprised. Ashley was delighted. She rode her new bike around the neighborhood, waving and smiling and calling "hello" to all her neighbors.

The neighbors were surprised. The neighbors were delighted. Everyone waved and smiled right back.

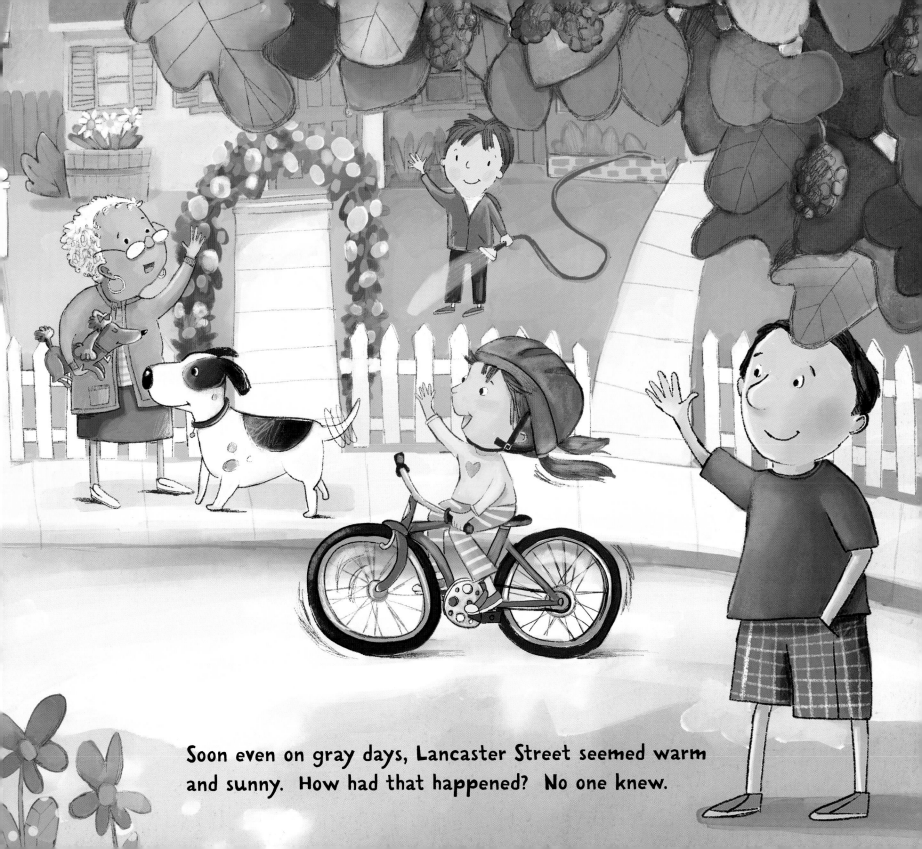

Soon even on gray days, Lancaster Street seemed warm and sunny. How had that happened? No one knew.

Not even Jake realized that it had all begun with a basket of mulberries and one mitzvah—one good deed.

## The Jewish Commandment to Do a Mitzvah

Love and kindness have been a part of Judaism from the very beginning. As the Torah says: "Love your neighbor as yourself." A large part of Jewish law is about treating people with kindness. In fact, acts of kindness are so much a part of Jewish behavior that the Hebrew word "mitzvah," which literally means "commandment," is often used to refer to a good deed.

## About Author and Illustrator

The author of over twenty children's books, Terri Fields has won numerous awards for her writing, including recognition from the American Library Association. Also a teacher, Terri has been named to the All USA Teacher Team of the nation's top teachers. She lives in Arizona.

A freelance illustrator in the San Francisco Bay area, Deborah Melmon has illustrated greeting cards, cookbooks, children's books, and playful educational materials, as well as environmental art for the California Science Museum. Among her book illustration projects are *Picnic at Camp Shalom* and *Speak Up, Tommy*.